friends

rain

window

flowers

birds

Monkey

umbrella

van

T-shirt

pants

socks

bread

string

paper

red box

blue box

yellow box

sails

anchor

backpack

compass

telescope

raincoat

boots

rain hat

ocean liner

submarine

boat

turtles

seals

necklaces

red jewels

pearls

green jewels

sandwiches

thermos

lightning

dolphins

fish

bathtub

soap

towel

A DK PUBLISHING BOOK

Project Editor Miriam Farbey
Art Editor Jane Thomas
Managing Editor Sheila Hanly
US Editor Camela Decaire
Illustrators Judith Moffatt, Gail Armstrong
Production Louise Barratt
Photography Dave King
Additional photography Andy Crawford, Steve Gorton,
Susanna Price, Tim Ridley

First American Edition, 1995
4 6 8 10 9 7 5

Published in the United States by
DK Publishing, Inc., 95 Madison Avenue
New York, New York 10016

Visit us on the World Wide Web at
http://www.dk.com

Library of Congress Cataloging-in-Publication Data

Davis, Lee. 1941–
    P.B. bear's treasure hunt / by Lee Davis. — 1st American ed.
        p.   cm.
    Summary: When Uncle Swashbuckler gives P.B. a map and key to a
secret treasure, P.B. and friends sail away to find the hidden
jewels and coins. Told in rebus form.
    ISBN 0-7894-0214-9
    1. Rebuses. [1. Teddy bears—Fiction. 2. Buried treasure–
–Fiction. 3. Rebuses.] I. Title.
PZ7.D29465Pag 1995
[E]—dc20   95-5466
                                                               CIP
                                                               AC

Color reproduction by Colourscan, Singapore
Printed and bound in Italy by L.E.G.O.

Acknowledgments

Dorling Kindersley would like to thank the following manufacturers
for permission to photograph copyright material:
Merrythought Ltd. for the parrot and the monkey
Margaret Steiff GmbH for the birds (p.6/7)
Ty Inc. for "Toffee" Style 2013 the dog
Carter and Parker Ltd. (Wendy Wools) for the Octopus pattern
Vera Small Designs for the sheep and lamb

Dorling Kindersley would also like to thank the following people for their help
in producing this book: Shaila Awan, Mike Buckley, Elizabeth Fitzgibbon, Tim Lewis,
Simon Money, Hannah Moseley, Barbara Owen, and Stephen Raw.

Can you find me
in each scene?

P.B. BEAR'S
TREASURE HUNT

Lee Davis

DK

One morning, P.B.  woke up early. He could

hear the  pattering against his . He looked

out and saw that the  were very wet.

"We're soaked through!" called some .

"Don't bother to come out until the  shines."

"Oh good!" said . "I have to stay inside.

That means I can wear my  a little bit longer."

But just as  snuggled back into ,

he heard a loud knock at the . He put on his

 and his  and hurried to open it.

"A big  for Mr. P.B.!" said Mailman .

"Thank you," said . "What awful weather!"

"Take your if you go out," said , and

he climbed into his and drove away.

"I'll get dressed and eat breakfast

before I open this," said .

He put on his , his

, and his . Then

he ate some and .

Just as  finished his breakfast there was another knock at the . When he opened it, there stood his friends Dermott and Pattie .

"Hello, ," said . "We thought you'd still be in on such a rainy day. Why did you get up?"

"I've just received a big ," answered .

"I don't know what's inside.

Can you guess?"

"Maybe it's a  from Auntie to fly to the ."

"Or a from Uncle to take us to the ."

What do *you* think is in the ?

 untied the  and tore off the  .

Inside the was a big red  , and inside

that was a blue , and inside that was a yellow  .

When looked in the red  , he found

some , an , and a  .

"We can build a with these," said  ,

"but I wonder what it's for?"

"Let's look in the other boxes for clues," said  .

They found an  in the blue and a 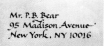 in

the yellow . Then opened the and took

out a , a , and a  . He read the

 out loud to his friends.

"Come on! Let's get

"You two build the [boat], and I'll pack

[compass] and a [flashlight] to help them find

"Is there enough food for all three of us?"

Next [teddy bear] put on his [shirt], his

the [pirate picture], and the [key]

ready to go!" shouted  .

my  ," said  . He packed a

their way. Then he packed food for a picnic.

asked  . Can you help her count?

 , and his  . He put the  ,

in his pocket. "Let's set sail!" he cried.

The  launched the  in the river. Soon the  stopped, the  came out, and a  appeared. They sailed past a farm. "Baa baa," said the . "We've lost our baby !" Can you help the  find the ?

They sailed past a 🏰 . "Have a good trip," said the 👑 and the 👑 . Soon they reached the mouth of the river, where they sailed past a 🚥 and out to sea.

"I'll use the  to find the island," said .

"Look! I can see an , a , and a ."

"There's a pair of friendly waving at us," cried ,

"and there are four and a huge !"

"I can spot 1 2 3 4 5 [seagulls]," barked [dog].

"One [seagull] has landed on top of a [palm tree]," said [bear].

"That must be the island where the treasure is buried."

The [boat] soon reached the shore.

Help  follow the clues to Oliver , who guards the treasure.

Hunt for the biggest shell on the island.

Look for four palm trees that hide what you seek.

Now cross over the bridge to Bear Island.

showed the 🏴‍☠️ to 🐙.

"At last!" said 🐙. "Let's dig up the 📦, then you can take me home with you."

🐻 dug with his 🪏 until he uncovered the 📦. He unlocked the lid with the 🗝️.

Lots of 🪙 and 📿 spilled out.

"Can you see four red 💎?" asked 🦜.

"Look for six 🔘 for me," barked 🐕.

"Find eight green 💎 for me," said 🐙.

"Let's take our favorite things and send the rest to Great-Uncle Swashbuckler," said 🐻. What would *you* take?

The  took the back to the .

"I'm hungry after all that digging," said . "Let's have

a picnic." They unpacked the , the ,

and the . After they had eaten the picnic,

collected , and played catch with a .

Then used his and

to build an enormous .

It was time for the  to go home.

As they set sail, the ☀ went behind a ☁,

the 💧💧 came pouring down, and ⚡⚡ flashed.

"Don't be scared of the storm," called some 🐬.

"Follow us!" cried some 🐠. "We'll show you the way."

At last, the reached P.B.'s house and said good-bye.

When  got home, he took off his [hat] , his [boots] , and his [shirt] . Then he took off his [striped shirt] , his [shorts] , and his [socks] . He climbed into his [bathtub] and scrubbed himself all over with [soap] .

He dried his fur with a [towel] and put on his favorite clothes, his [pajamas] . Then he was ready to climb into his favorite place, [bed] .

Can you count the things he brought home from his journey?

Good night, [bear] !

P.B. Bear   Dermott   Pattie   Oliver

Sun   pajamas   bed   door   bathrobe   slippers   package

honey   rocket   Astronaut   Moon   car   Clown   circus

flag   sailboat   envelope   key   letter   photograph   map

rainbow   sheep   lamb   castle   King   Queen   lighthouse

whale   seagulls   palm tree   treasure chest   shovel   coins

apples   shells   crab   bucket   sand castle   cloud